RUBBERS
Written and Penciled by Erich Onzik
Inked by Jeffrey Priester

<u>TABLE OF CONTENTS</u>

<u>ACKNOWLEDGMENTS</u>

This book is dedicated to all the people who helped me along the way. Mom, Dad, Sisters, Brothers, Jeffrey Priester, Ian Kent, Ex-girlfriends past and future and, of course, all those lovesick drunks out there.

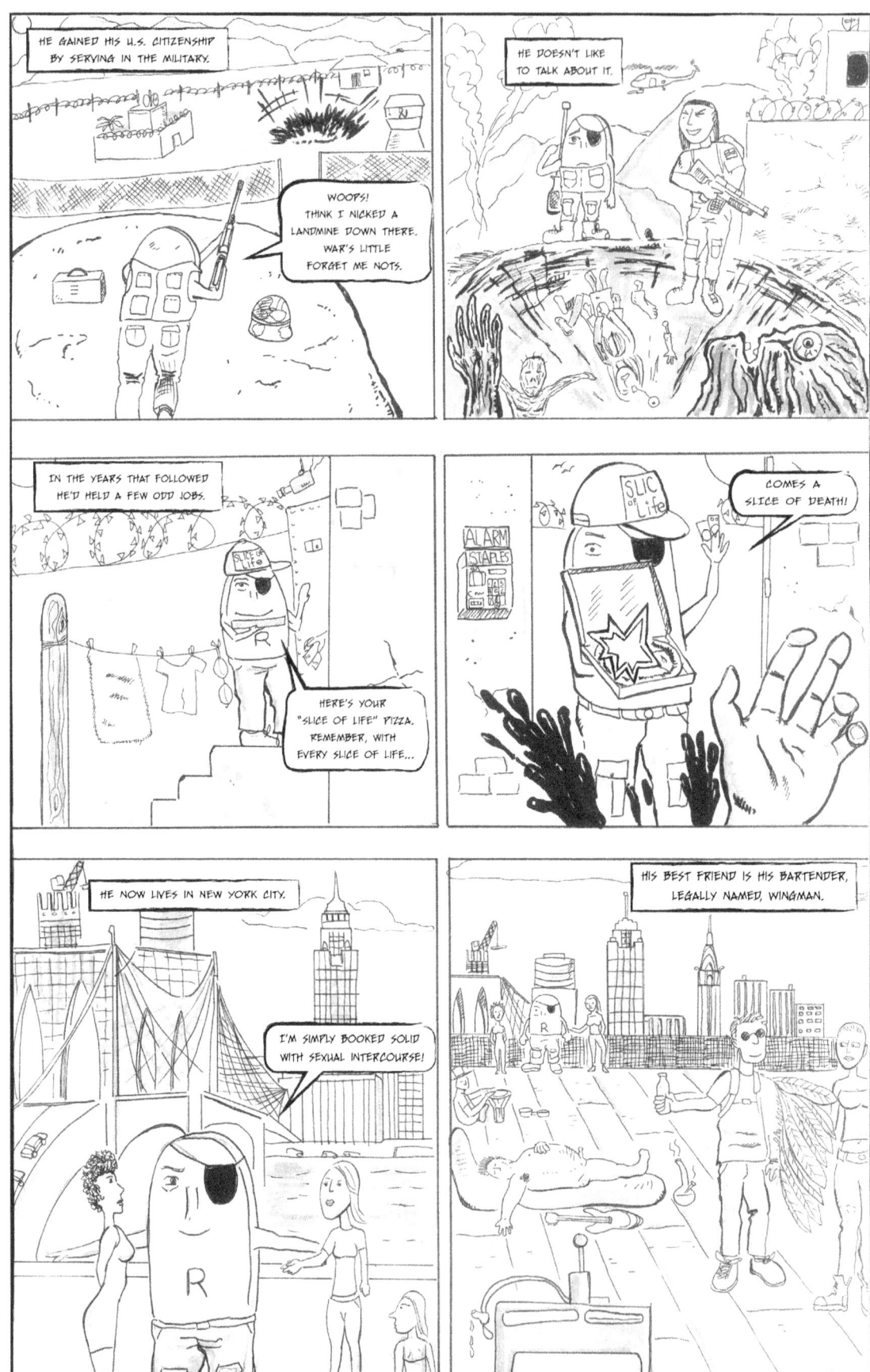

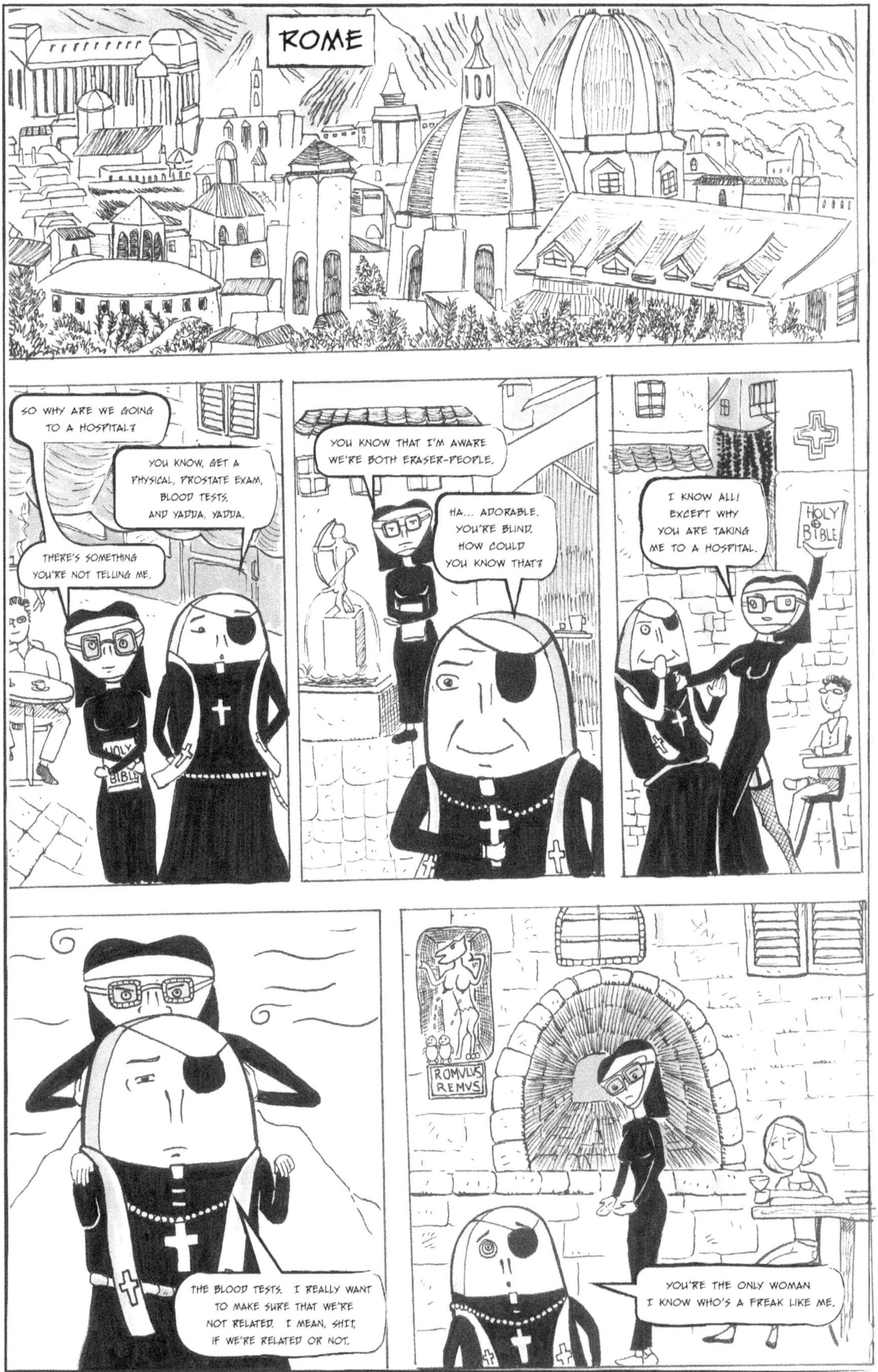

AWAY WE GO I HOPE. I HEAR POLICE BOATS. YOU'VE MADE ME AN ACCOMPLICE!
MY SEXY- I MEAN MY SECRET ACCOMPLICE. WERE YOU WORKING FOR ME ALL ALONG?
PensIAMo SOGGETTO e AMERICANO!
R
TRANSLATED BY G**GLE, THEN TRANSLATED BACK.
SHOOT TO WOUND THESE FATS, SMUGGLING, AMERICAN, TOURISTS.
POLIZIA
LET'S GET THE HELL OUT OF HERE.
FAIR ENOUGH. HOW ABOUT ROME? PLENTY OF PLACES TO HIDE THERE.
UH...
R
THEY'RE OPENING FIRE! PERCHÉ, YOU ASSHOLES?!
UVA
STATUARY
R
WE SHOT THE PERSON SQUARE, AND NOW THE BOAT CONTINUES WITHOUT HIM.
RETRIEVE THE BODY!
MERDA!
U.S. COAST GUARD
SHARKSKIN
VA FF AN CU LO

CLARA

THE

RUBBER

MAIDEN

CLARA WAS DISCOVERED ON EASTER ISLAND
BY THE RAPA NUI TRIBE.
THOUGH SHE WAS BORN BLIND
SHE KNEW THEY WORSHIPPED AND LOVED HER.

SHE WAS LATER ADOPTED BY A FAMILY
WHO RAN A COMMUNE OF SATANISTS
AND GREW WEED IN THE FORESTS OF NORTHERN CALIFORNIA.

SHE GRADUATED MAGNA CUM LAUDE
WITH A DEGREE IN ANTHROPOLOGY.

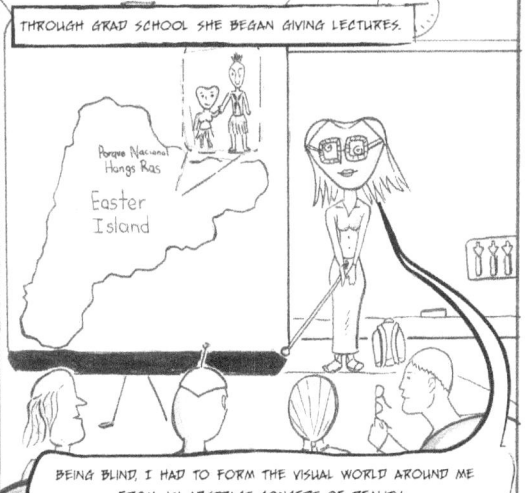

THROUGH GRAD SCHOOL SHE BEGAN GIVING LECTURES.

BEING BLIND, I HAD TO FORM THE VISUAL WORLD AROUND ME
FROM AN ABSTRACT CONCEPT OF REALITY.
YET I PERCEIVE THINGS WITH A SORT OF CLAIRAUDIENCE.
I'VE LEARNT TO PERCEIVE HUMANITY'S GROWTH
BY LISTENING TO THEIR WAVERING TONES OF VOICE, TO THEIR SONG.
AND MAKING LOVE TO THEM FROM TIME TO TIME.

BUT I PICK UP SIGNIFICANTLY MORE WITH MY ENLARGED PINEAL GLAND.
STUDYING YOU SOCIALLY, ECONOMICALLY, SPIRITUALLY,
SEXUALLY, AND ANTHROPOLOGICALLY, THROUGH THE MIND'S EYE.
SO... HELLO THERE... WANT TO SHAKE MY HAND?

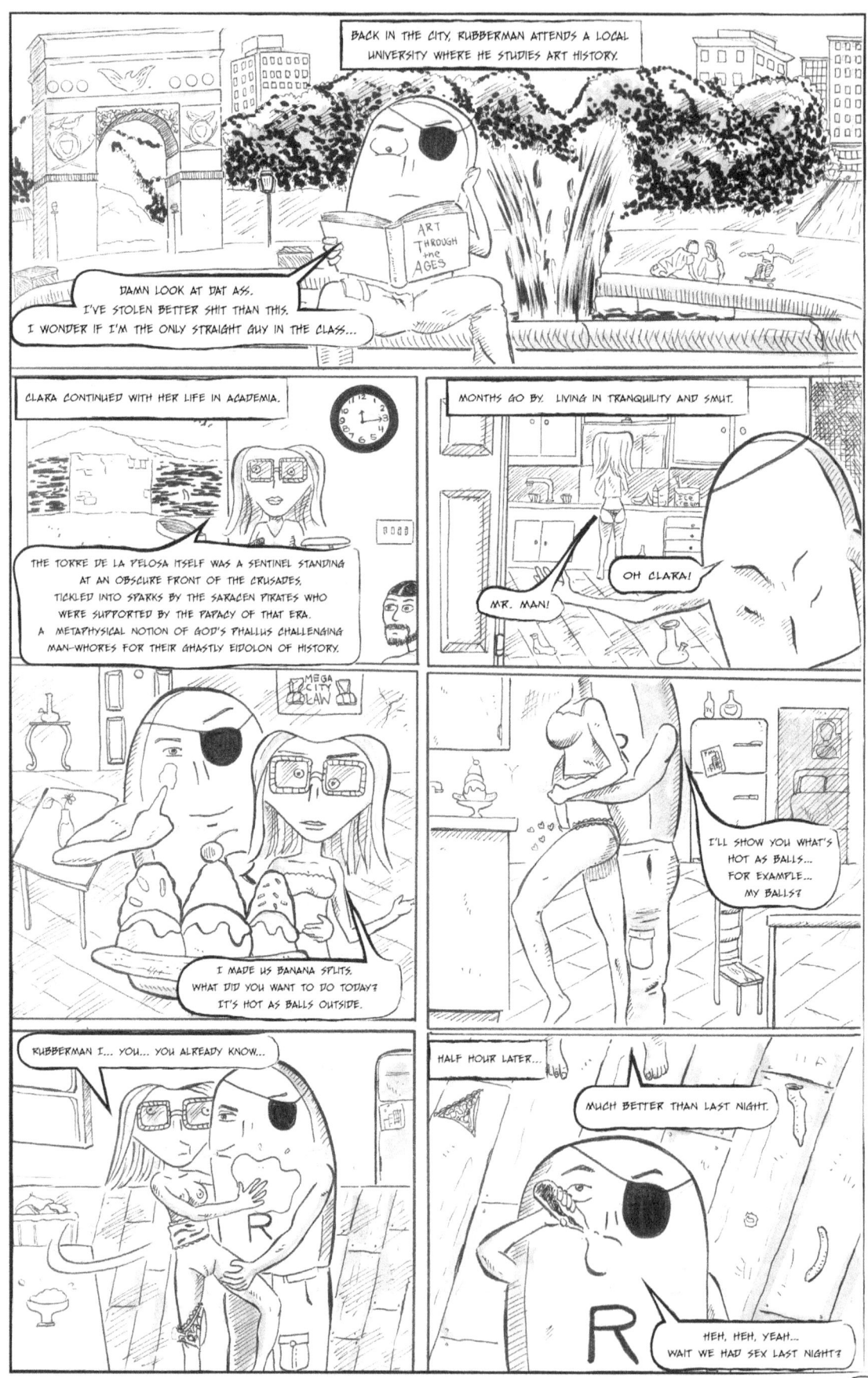

(17)

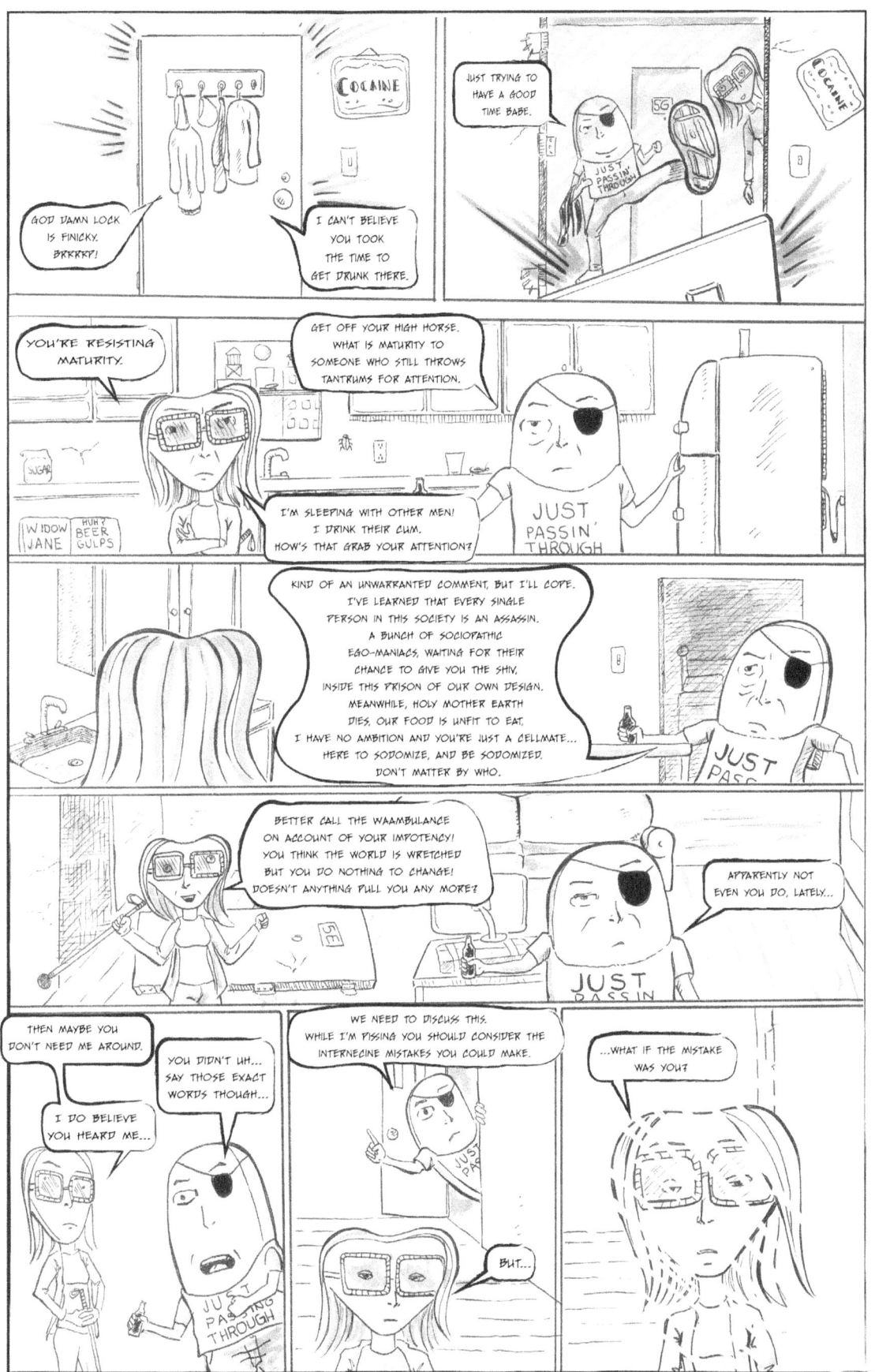

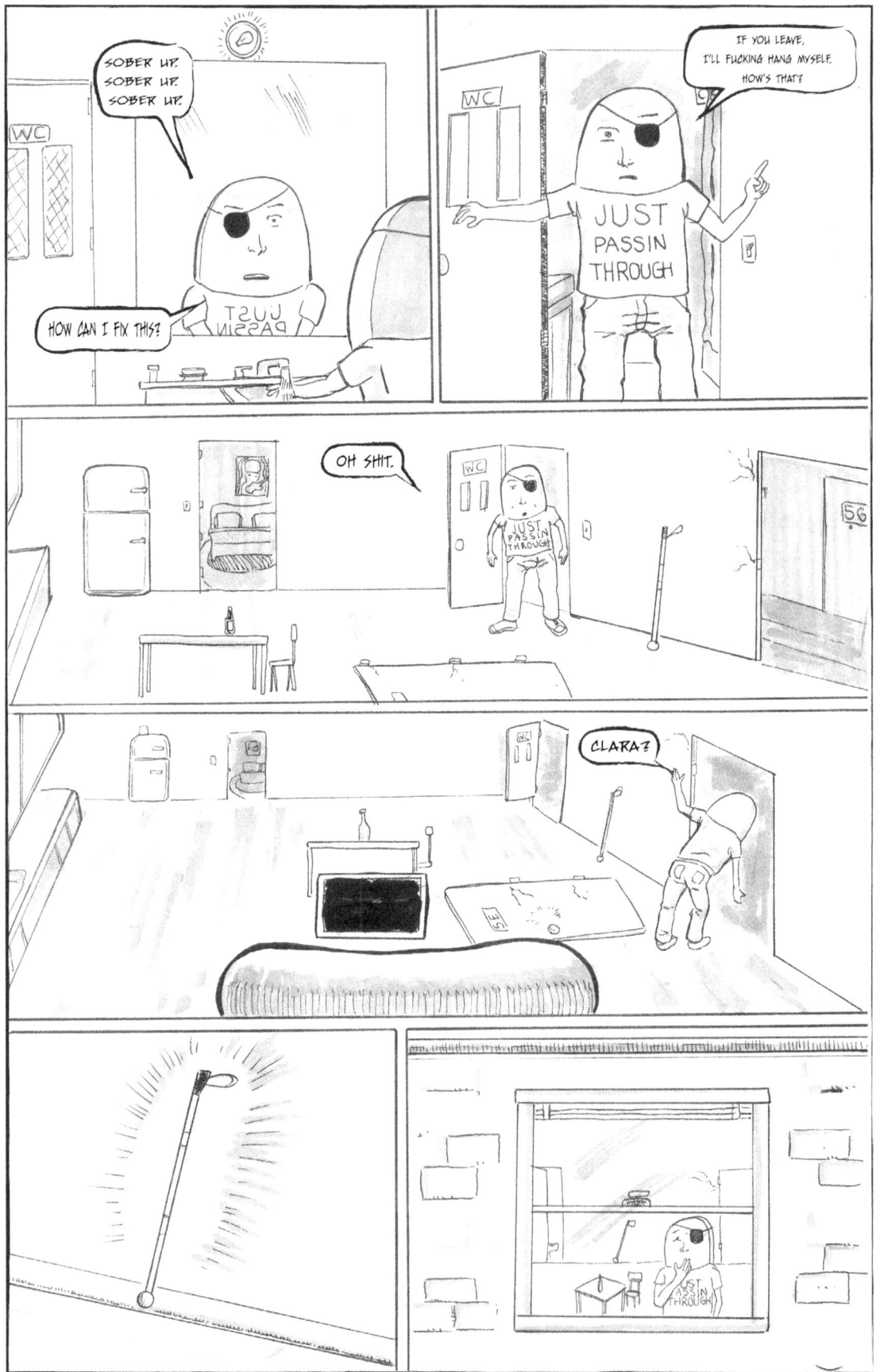

WEEKS LIKE MENSTRUATING SLUGS.

BLOATED WITH TOXIN, A BASTED TURKEY GENERATES HIS OWN HEAT.

IN THE HYPNAPOMPIC STATE AFTER DRUNKEN SLEEP, ANXIOUS THOUGHTS RUMINATE UNFORGIVINGLY.

NOBODY AROUND TO MAKE SURE MY PENIS WORKS EXCEPT ME

I'M CONVINCED THE SIXTH OR SEVENTH TIME IN A DAY IS STILL JUST KEEPING PACE WITH EVERYONE ELSE.

LET'S GO SEE IF JENNA HAZE WILL LET US IN FOR SOME POOLSIDE FUCKIN'.

AH... OK... YEAH...

SO WHAT'S UP JENNA? YOU READY FOR SOME... POOLSIDE FUCKIN'?

NO, ACTUALLY. IT'S MY DAY OFF.

OH. ARRIGHT THEN.

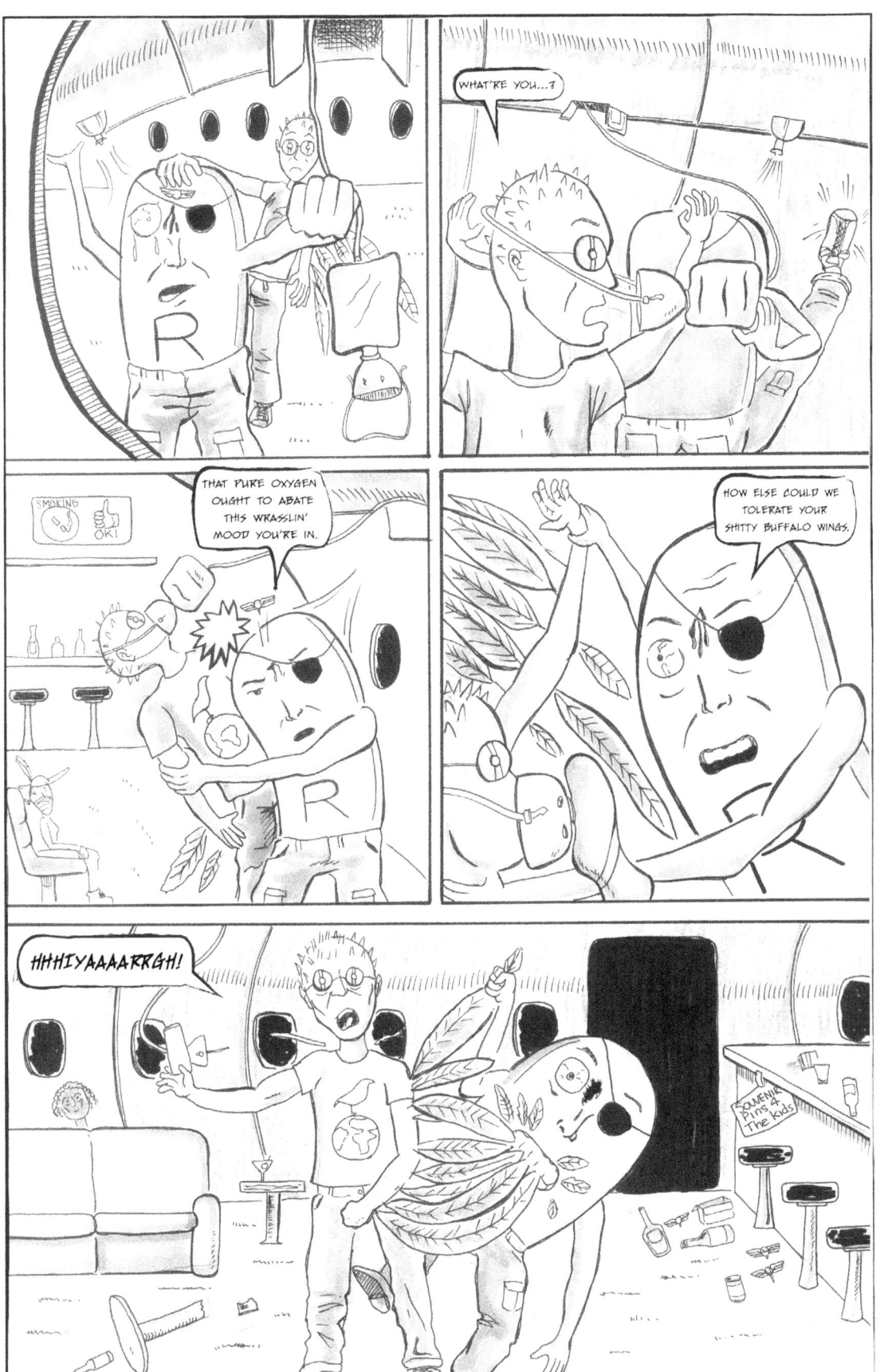

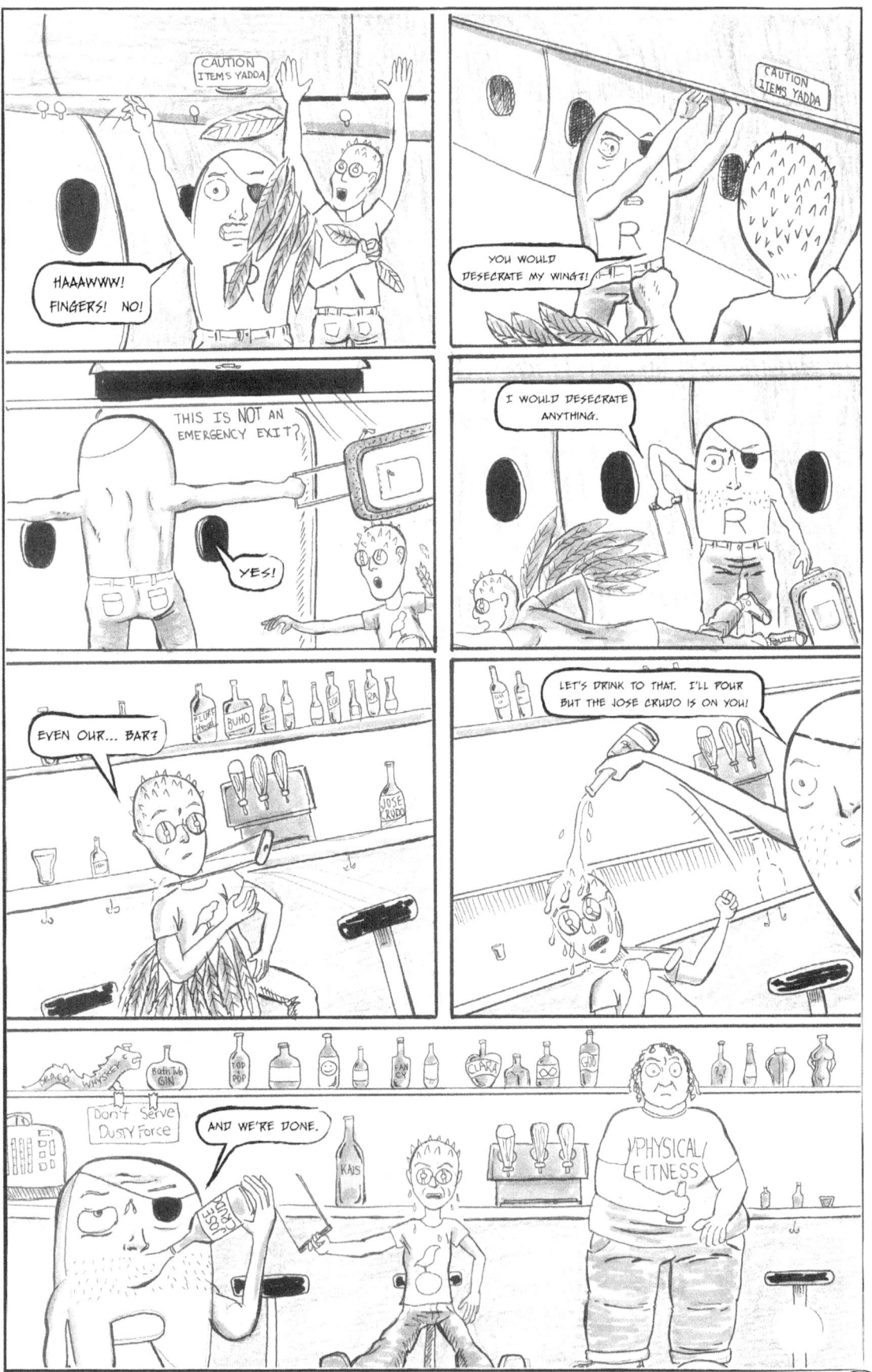

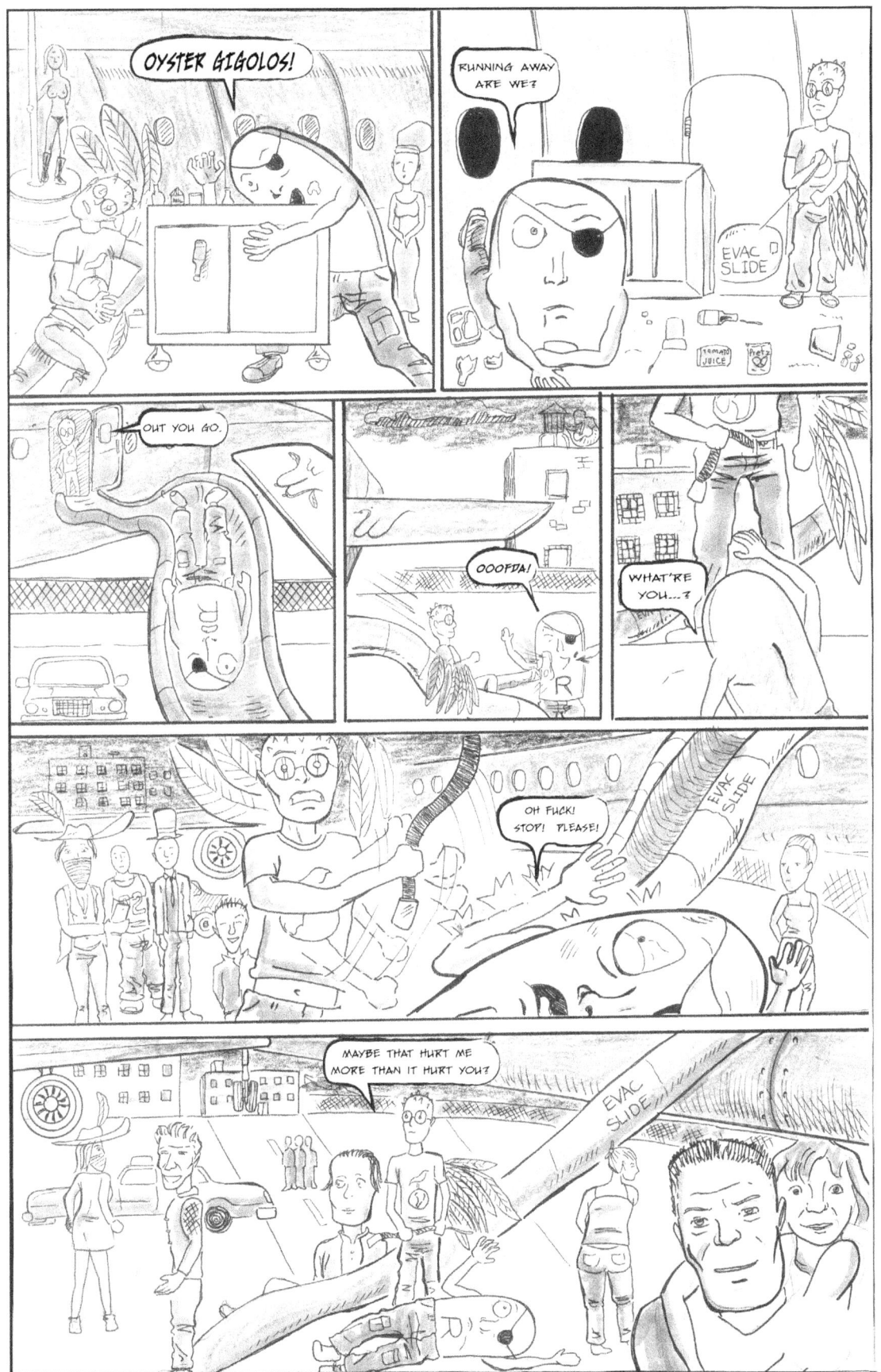

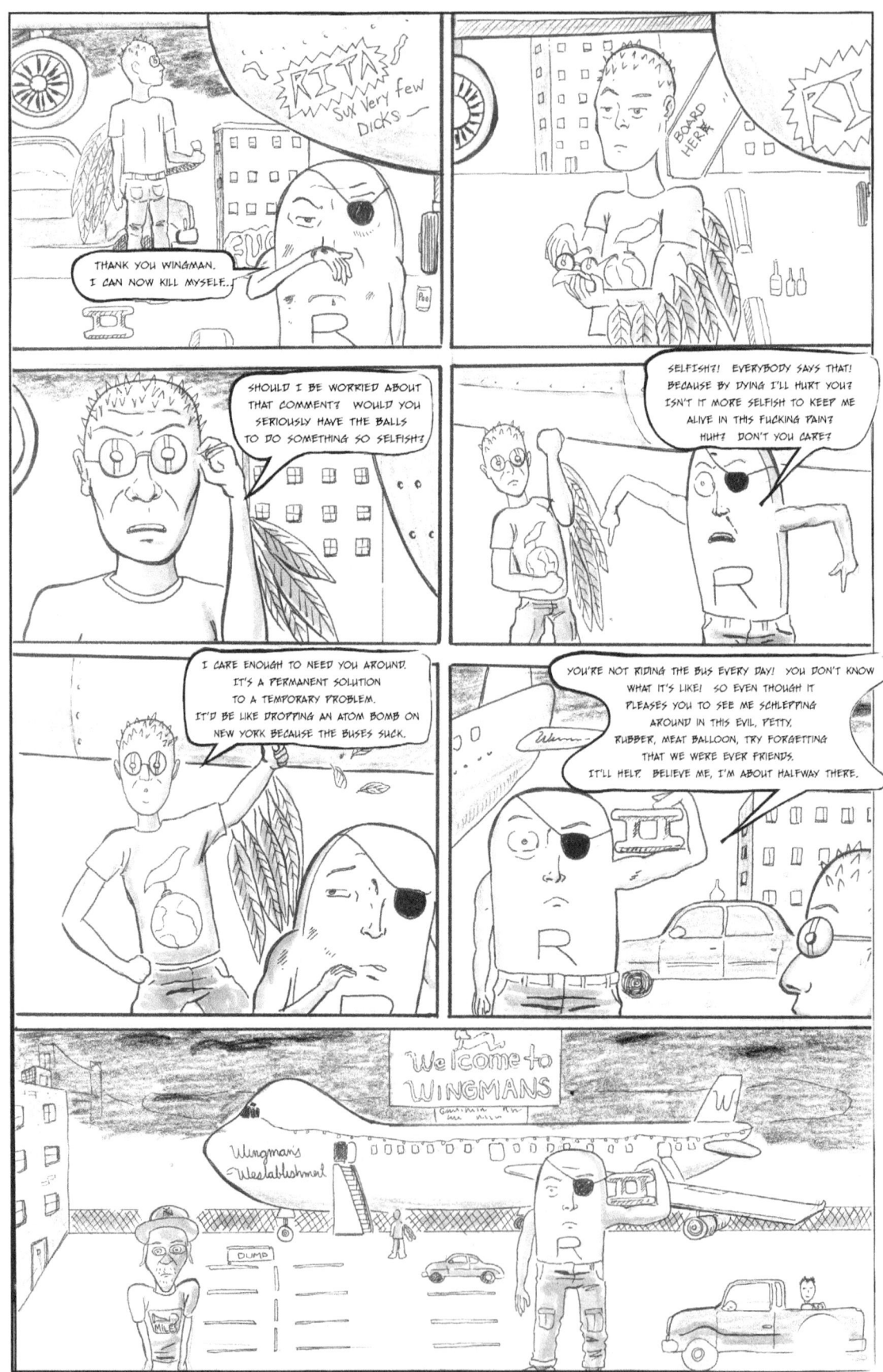

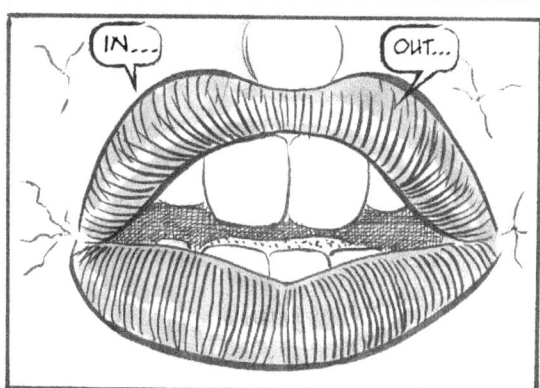

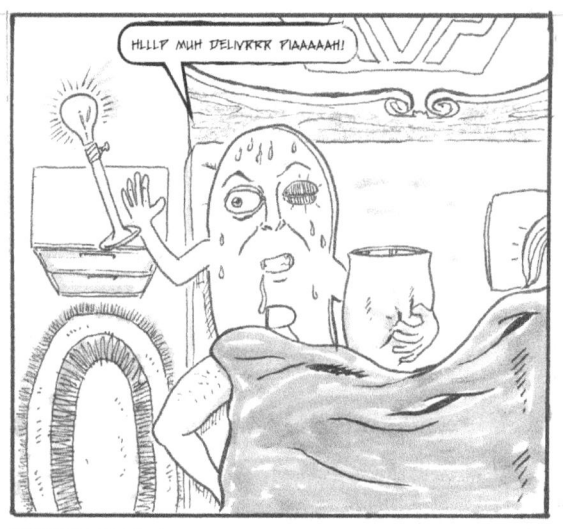

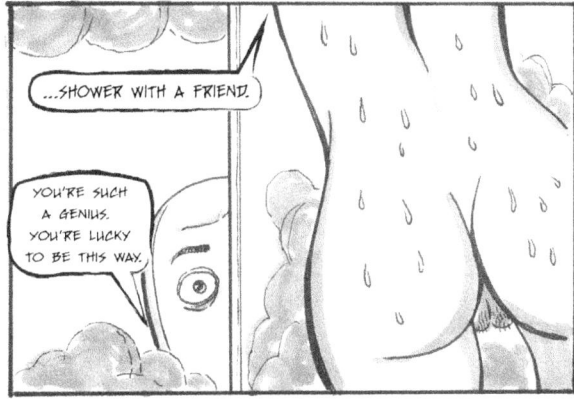

I KNOW (I KNOW) YOU BELOOOOOONG TO SOOOOOMEBODY NEEEEEW...

...BUT TONIIIGHT YOU BELOOONG TO ME... YADDA YADDA.

YOU! YOU'RE INVITED TO STAY ON MY PROPERTY IF YOU WANT ANOTHER HARSH LESSON IN MANNERS!

I COME IN PEACE, YOU ASSHOLE.

CHOOSE YOUR NEXT WORDS WISELY RUBBS, BEFORE I "BEAT THEE INTO HANDSOMENESS."

ALRIGHT THEN. I COMPULSIVELY MASTURBATE TO THE POINT OF CHAFFING, I TRIED TO COMMIT SUICIDE WITH A CINDER BLOCK, I FUCKED MY EX-GIRLFRIEND ALL OF YESTERDAY ONLY TO SEE HER KIDNAPPED BY ANOTHER, PRETTIER, AND PROBABLY MORE MOTIVATED VERSION OF MYSELF, FROM ANOTHER DIMENSION. IN A FURY, I ACCIDENTALLY BLEW UP MY APARTMENT JUST AS SOME RANDOM F.B.I.-SWAT TEAM BROKE IN. LATER, I TRIED HAVING PHONE SEX WITH MEGAN FROM THE SUICIDE HOTLINE.

HEH HEH. HOLY SHIT. HAHA.

HELP... PLEASE HELP?

WINGMAN! GOOD GOD, WHAT HAPPENED THERE?

AH! MY FATHER'S GHOST AGAIN... ACID FLASHBACK.

NOW THAT THAT'S OVER WE CAN OFFICIALLY BEGIN ANEW, PUTTING ALL APPALLING INCIDENTS BEHIND US. WINGMAN I WROTE YOU A POEM...

AH-AH-HEM. WINGMAN, I THINK IN MANY WAYS OUR FIST FIGHT BROUGHT US CLOSER TOGETHER. BUT WE SHOULD NOT DO IT AGAIN ANYTIME SOON. YOU ARE NOT JUST MY BARTENDER BUT, INDUBITABLY, THE ONLY MAN I CAN OPEN MY MIND TO, EVEN WHEN HE DOESN'T WANT ME TO. BUT AT LEAST WE CAN AGREE THAT WE HATE THE PEOPLE WHO WATCH SPORTS RERUNS AT THE BAR. I HATE THOSE PEOPLE. I'M SORRY THAT I'M A BAD, BEST FRIEND.

THAT WAS NOT A POEM.

BZZZZ

BUT ANYWAYS, ENOUGH ROMANCE. LET'S SOFTEN OUR HEARTS AND HARDEN OUR LIVERS BY DRINKING TO THE BYGONES AND TO THE FORTHCOMING.

HERE! HERE!

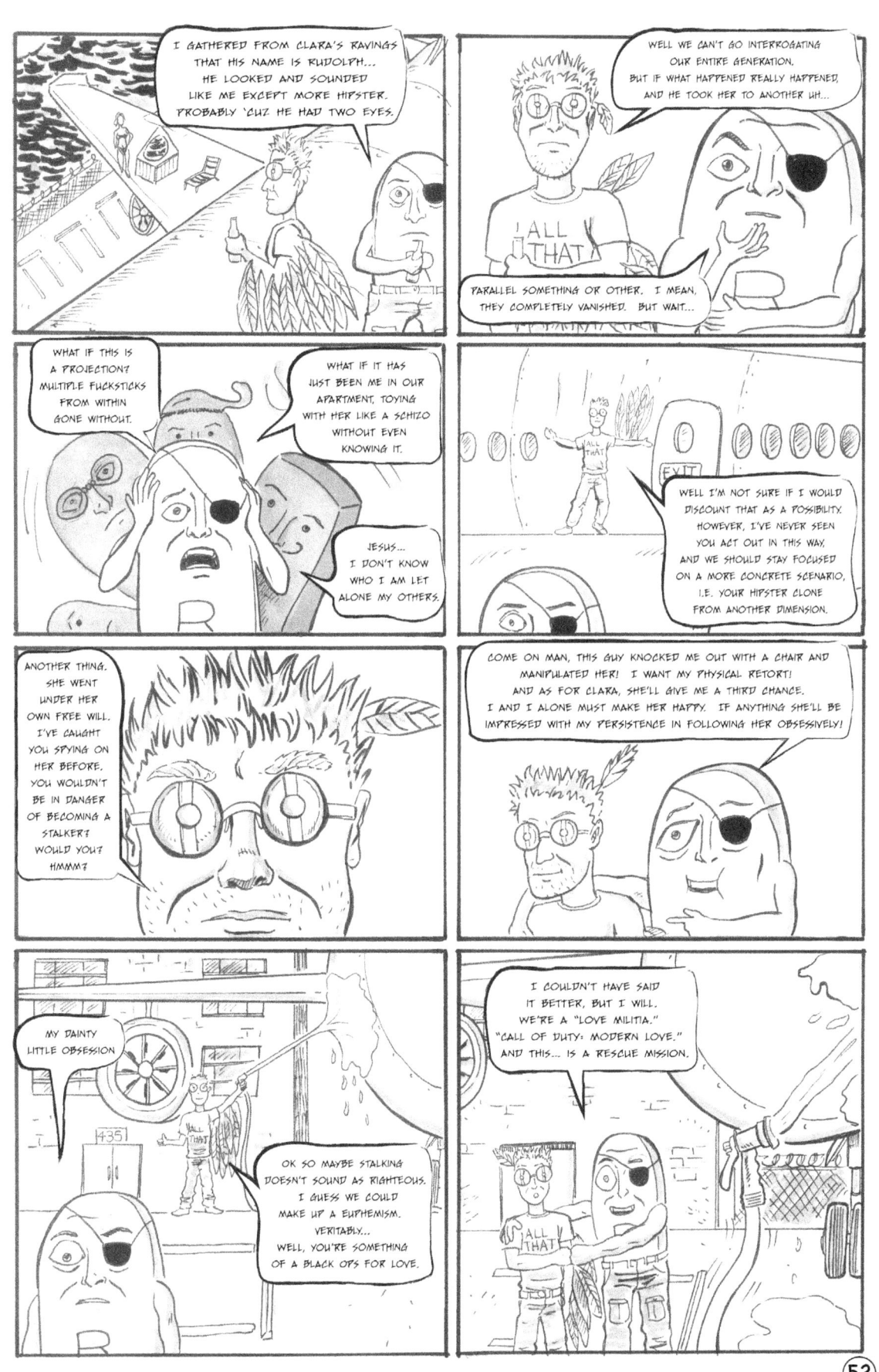

Westablishment

MY GOD. IT'S KIND OF MARVELOUS ISN'T IT?

IT'S NOT THE SOUNDEST OF INVESTMENTS, AND ACCORDING TO MY SPHINCTER I REMAIN UNIMPRESSED. WE'VE ALL SEEN AIRCRAFT BEFORE.

WE GO IN INCOGNITO. SAX... WITH ALL THE SHIT THAT'S GONE DOWN, HE COULD BE PUNISHABLE FOR KIDNAPPING, MURDER, HE MIGHT BE BUILDING A BOMB SOMEWHERE, OR WORSE YET, AN ENERGY RESOURCE FOR THE MASSES THAT OUR SPONSORS MIGHT NOT APPRECIATE. I WANT THIS CASE CLOSED DELICATELY AND INFALLIBLY.

MY MOTHER AND FATHER USED TO TELL ME STORIES ABOUT YOU AND THEM DOING THIS TYPE OF STUFF.

THEY HAD INCREDIBLE CAREERS BEFORE THEY PASSED, YOUNG SAX. IT SEEMED LIKE EVERYTHING CAME SO EASY TO THEM. THEIR DISTASTE FOR HIPPIE RADICALS WAS AS PROFOUND AS THEIR AFFECTION FOR EACH OTHER. I EVEN STATED THAT IN THEIR EULOGY.

IN THE END I BELIEVE THAT'S THE REASON WHY THEY DID THEIR JOBS SO WELL, WHY ANY OF US DO. IT'S FOR THE LOVE OF OUR FAMILIES, AND THE LOVE OF OUR FELLOW AMERICANS, COUPLED WITH ANTIPATHY FOR LAZINESS. FOR WE THE PEOPLE CAN ONLY LOVE SO MUCH. GAME FACES NOW.

OKAY... EVERYBODY SHUT THE FUCK UP... PLEASE. I'VE GOT A PROPOSITION FOR YOU BARFLIES.

THAT MUST BE THE OWNER OF THE BAR UP THERE, WINGMAN.

WHERE THE HELL IS THE ERASER MAN?

THE TRAIN IS STOPPED DUE TO TRAFFIC AHEAD OF US. WE ARE SORRY FOR ANY INCONVENIENCE. WE HAVE NO CHOICE BUT TO BE SORRY. WE WILL ALWAYS BE SORRY BECAUSE EVENTUALLY WE WILL ALWAYS LET SOMEBODY DOWN. IF YOU DON'T LEARN TO APPRECIATE THE MTA FOR IT'S FAULTS, THEN YOU ARE NOT WORTHY OF US EITHER.

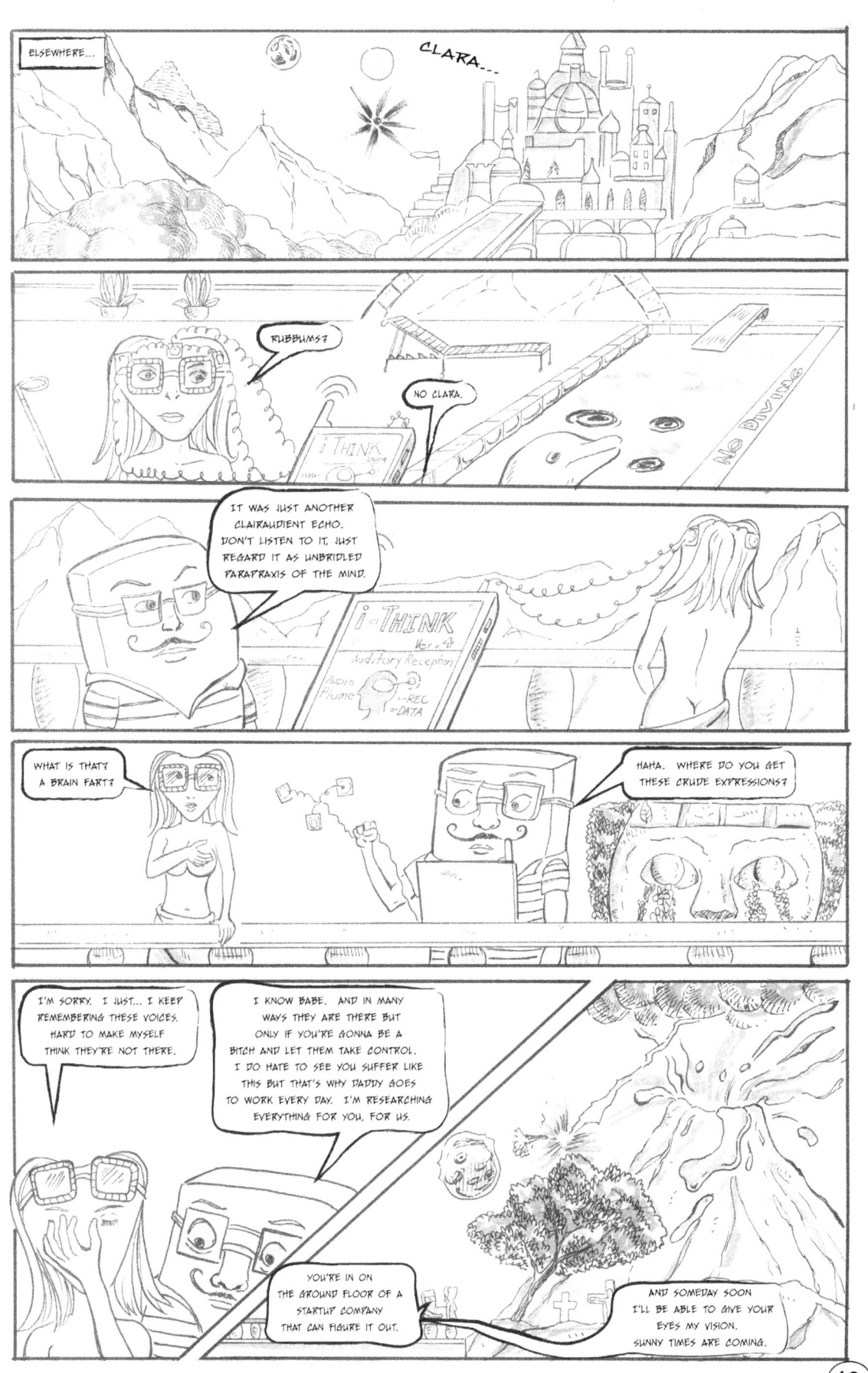

IT'S UNBELIEVEABLE ELOI. THESE PEOPLE MUST HAVE NOTHING BETTER TO DO THAN TO SUPPORT MY CAUSE IN EXCHANGE FOR FREE BOOZE. MERCENARIES IN MY "LOVE MILITIA" PAID WITH BEER, WINE, AND SPIRIT, ER... SPIRITS.

I FEEL STRANGE AMONGST SUCH LURID DRUNKS.

WHAT? I THOUGHT YOU CAME HERE ALL THE TIME.

I NORMALLY ONLY COME HERE TO GET BLACKOUT AND PRETEND I DON'T EXIST. TONIGHT IS PARTICULARLY HORRENDOUS. I THINK THAT ONE'S TRYING TO ESTABLISH DOMINANCE.

SO WE'RE HERE. WHY WINGMAN? YOU WERE MY FAVORITE BARTENDER.

I'M SORRY IF MY FRIEND HURT YOU. BUT IF I'M NOT MISTAKEN WE NEED THE MIND OF A GENIUS.

FOR WHAT?

SOME DOPPELGANGER, ASSHOLE, BIRD-DOGGED ME AND TOOK MY WOMAN TO ANOTHER DIMENSION. FOR THE SAKE OF ALL THAT WE KNOW, WHICH IS TEETERING ON NOTHING, I NEED YOUR EXPERTISE. THAT IS... IF YOU ARE WHO WE THINK YOU ARE. WAIT, SO, WHO EXACTLY ARE YOU ELOI?

AUCH DU LIEBE.

I'LL TELL YOU THE COCKAMAMIE TRUTH AND THEN WE'LL JUDGE WHO'S WHO LATER. I'M FROM A STEP TO THE LEFT OF THIS MACROCOSM. YOU CAN CALL IT ANOTHER DIMENSION BUT IT'S NOT REALLY. IT'S A NEW PLAY WITH THE SAME ACTORS IN DIFFERENT ROLES.

I COME FROM AN EARTH THAT HAS NO "COUNTRIES," AS YOU CALL THEM, ONLY TERRITORIES RULED UNDER A CORPORATE-PROLETARIAT ELITE. THE MAIN ECONOMY WAS BASED SOLELY ON COCOA AND ITS DERIVATIVE PRODUCTS.

Cocoa-Cola
RATIONS →
← LABOR

I EARNED MY CHOCOLATE RATIONS AS A RENOWNED PHYSICIST. MY REPUTATION WAS CORNERSTONE TO MY ENTIRE FIELD.

Scientists Convicted of Manslaughter

BUT THROUGH SOME SEDITION OR ANOTHER, BIG COCOA RULED THE WORLD AND IT CORRUPTED ANY SOUND RESEARCH RESULTS WE HAD BY BUYING AND RUINING THE LIVES OF ANYBODY WHO STOOD OUT AS TOO SMART.

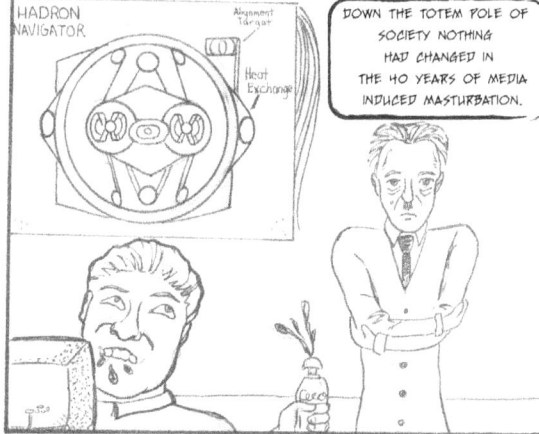

CHOCOLATE WASTE, CONVERTED BY E.COLI, RAN HYDROGEN FUEL CELLS IN POWER PLANTS AND VEHICLES. USEFUL AS IT WAS, OTHER GOOD IDEAS OUTSIDE THE COCOA TRADE WERE SHOT DOWN OR BOUGHT AND SMOTHERED BY THEIR POLITICAL CRONIES AT THE HELM OF THE WORLD ORDER.

HADRON NAVIGATOR
Alignment Target
Heat Exchange

DOWN THE TOTEM POLE OF SOCIETY NOTHING HAD CHANGED IN THE 40 YEARS OF MEDIA INDUCED MASTURBATION.

THE LAST SEVERAL YEARS WERE VERY TRYING. AN INFLUENTIAL COCOA BARON BEGAN SANCTIONING THE RATIONS FROM MYSELF AND MY FAMILY. MY FUNDING FOR HADRON TRANSPORTATION RESEARCH WAS KAPUT.

Cocoa Hut

IT WAS DEPRESSING FOR EVERYONE AND SOME TOOK IT HARD. PERHAPS TOO HARD.

CHOCOLATE FONDUE

THERE WERE MANY A CHOCOLATE COATED MARTYR IN THAT CORPORATE-COMMUNIST, COCOA, HELLHOLE.

CHOCOLATE FONDUE

A REFLECTION CAPTURES LIGHT.

AND GATHER'S AETHER'S FLOCK.

BLOODY SHITE...

TURN EAST HERE AND WE'VE DONE IT! HAHH! JUST PASSING THROUGH...

NO DIFFERENT THAN SMOKING CRACK REALLY...

HOW SORDIDLY ENLIGHTENING. THANK GOD NOTHING HORRIBLE HAPPENED.

DAMN YOU PEOPLE! TAKING THE SUPPOSITORY WASN'T JUST FOR MORALE.

WHO WAS HE?

HE WAS F.B.I. A SPECIAL AGENT NAMED CHAPMAN, AND I DO BELIEVE HE CAME WITH A LADY...

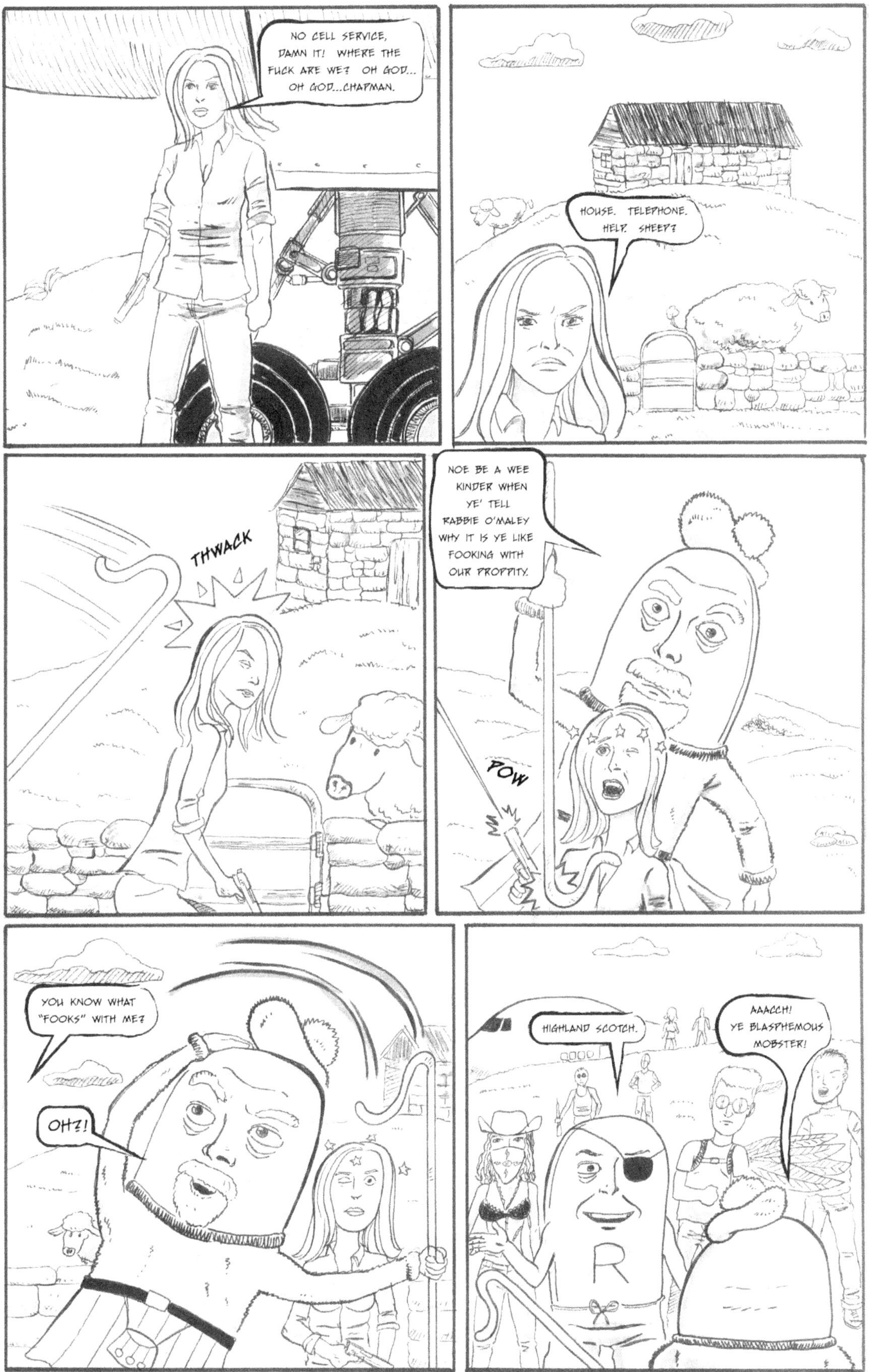

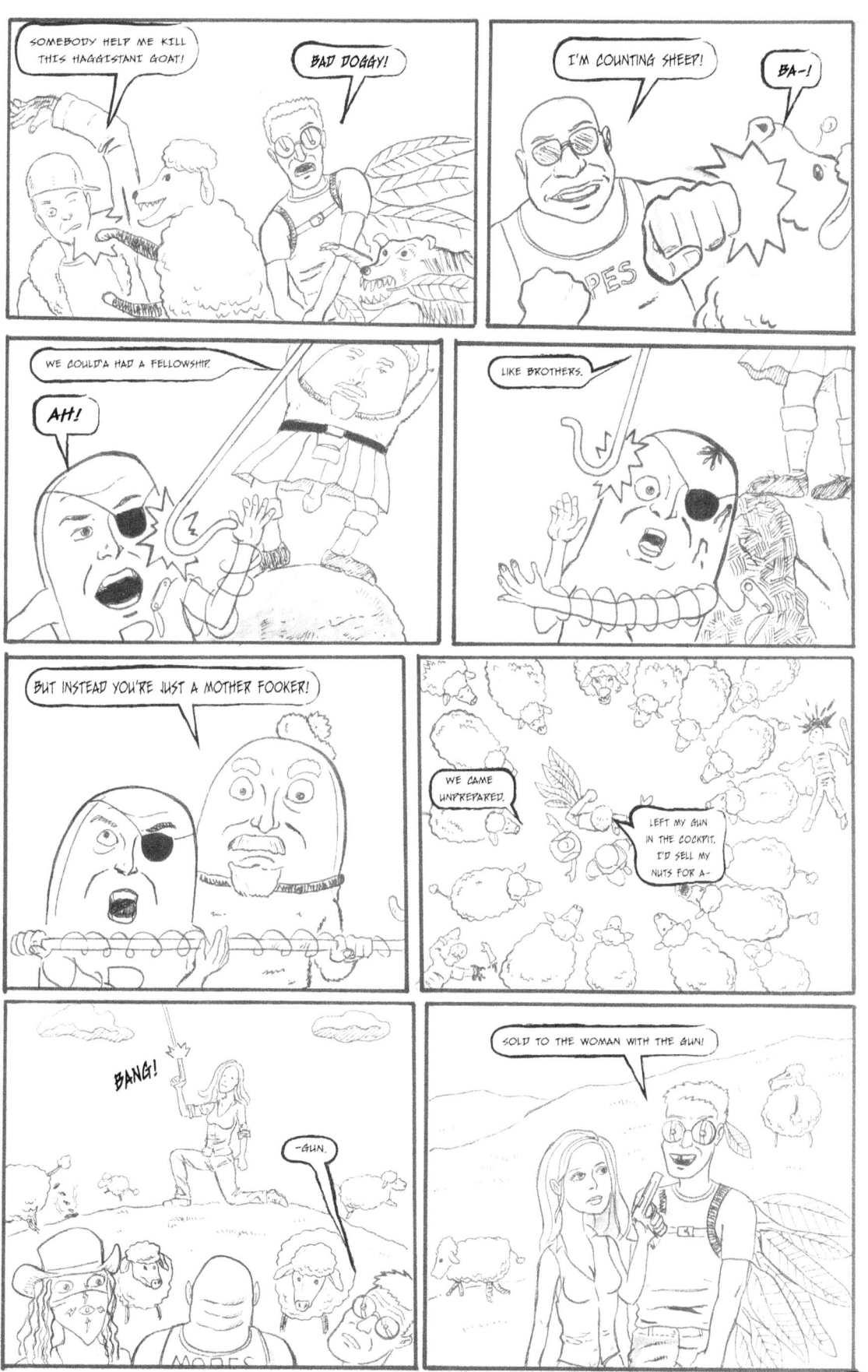

EYES GLASSY AND GREY AT THE SIGHT OF DEATH.

I LOVE HER TOO, YE KEN. EVEN AS MY HEART FAILS ME IT STILL BEATS FOR HER. OUR MAN, AND I DO MEAN OUR MAN, HAS HER LIKE A TROPHY. AND HE'S A SMART BASTARD HE IS. KNOWS ABOUT YOU, KNOWS ABOUT US ALL. SO WHY'D HE STEAL HER? WHO KENS? MAYBE HE T'INKS SHE LOVED YOU THE MOST... OR ME...

BUT WE'RE ALL JUST MURDEROUS WANKERS YE- HE- ME-*

GOOD LUCK ON THE OTHER SIDE YOU POOR, POOR, SHEEPFUCKER...

YOU THERE! YOU STILL JUST A COP?

I'M STILL JUST AN FBI AGENT IF THAT'S WHAT YOU MEAN.

NO, NOT JUST. YOU ARE ALSO KNOWN AS SHE WHO INDIRECTLY HELPED ME HASTEN THIS MAN TO HIS DOOM. WHICH MEANS YOU'RE INDIRECTLY RESPONSIBLE... YOU'RE LIKE WINGMAN, A BARTENDER HANDING A DRUNK HIS KEYS JUST SO HE CAN CLOSE DOWN EARLY.

AHEM... WELL...

ERR... WELL. MIND IF I DISARM YOU?

YOU ALREADY HAVE. FOR NOW...

HOW ODDLY EROTIC. BUT THAT'S PROBABLY MY DIAGNOSED "ODDLY EROTIC FIXATION" KICKING IN AGAIN.

MINDLESS PRATTLE...

ALRIGHT EVERYONE, BACK ON THE PLANE. GRAB SOME SHEEP. WE MAY ER... NEED THEM.

FARTHER INLAND...

RELEASE THE PIG CARCASSES!

NO IT'S NOT ALL ABOUT THE CHOCOLATE, DESPITE WHAT ELOI MIGHT HAVE TOLD YOU. IT'S ABOUT ECONOMIZING.

IT'S ABOUT BALANCE AND RESPECTING THE INTERCONNECTIVITY OF EVERYTHING. OUR COMRADES, THE CONSUMERS, SHARE THE BLESSINGS EQUALLY, AS WELL AS THE MISERIES. BUT TO BE MISERABLE IS TO BE MEAT.

THOSE OLD PIG CARCASSES WE COULDN'T SELL WILL GO TO THE WATER RESERVOIR.

IT'S NOT TOO OPTIMISTIC TO THINK WE COULD POISON A GREAT NUMBER OF PEOPLE BEFORE SOME COUNCILMAN HIRES OUR SISTER COMPANY IN WASTE DISPOSAL.

AND IF THE WATER DOESN'T AIL THEM, THEN SURELY OUR COCOA-FOOD AND COCOA-FUEL PRODUCTS WILL. WE OFFER THE PUBLIC A LARGE ARRAY OF CHOICES FOR THEIR PUBLICLY OWNED PRIVATELY RUN SELF DESTRUCTION.

AND THEY'LL GET THE MOST DESIRABLE CHOCOLATE PILLS FROM OUR DOCTORS TO HELP WITH THEIR INHERENT SICKNESS UNDER HEALTH INSURANCE THAT COVERS NOTHING FOR EVERYONE.

AND THEY'LL HAVE TO PAY FOR IT ALL BY WORKING FOR US. THIS WORLD'S TRUEST FORM OF A SYNERGISTIC-FUSION ECONOMY. IRREVOCABLE BALANCE THAT WE KNOW AND LOVE. ONE WE CAN PERPETUATE SO THAT EVERY GENERATION RELIES ON OUR SUCCESS. YOU SEE THEY... NEED ME TO SUCCEED.

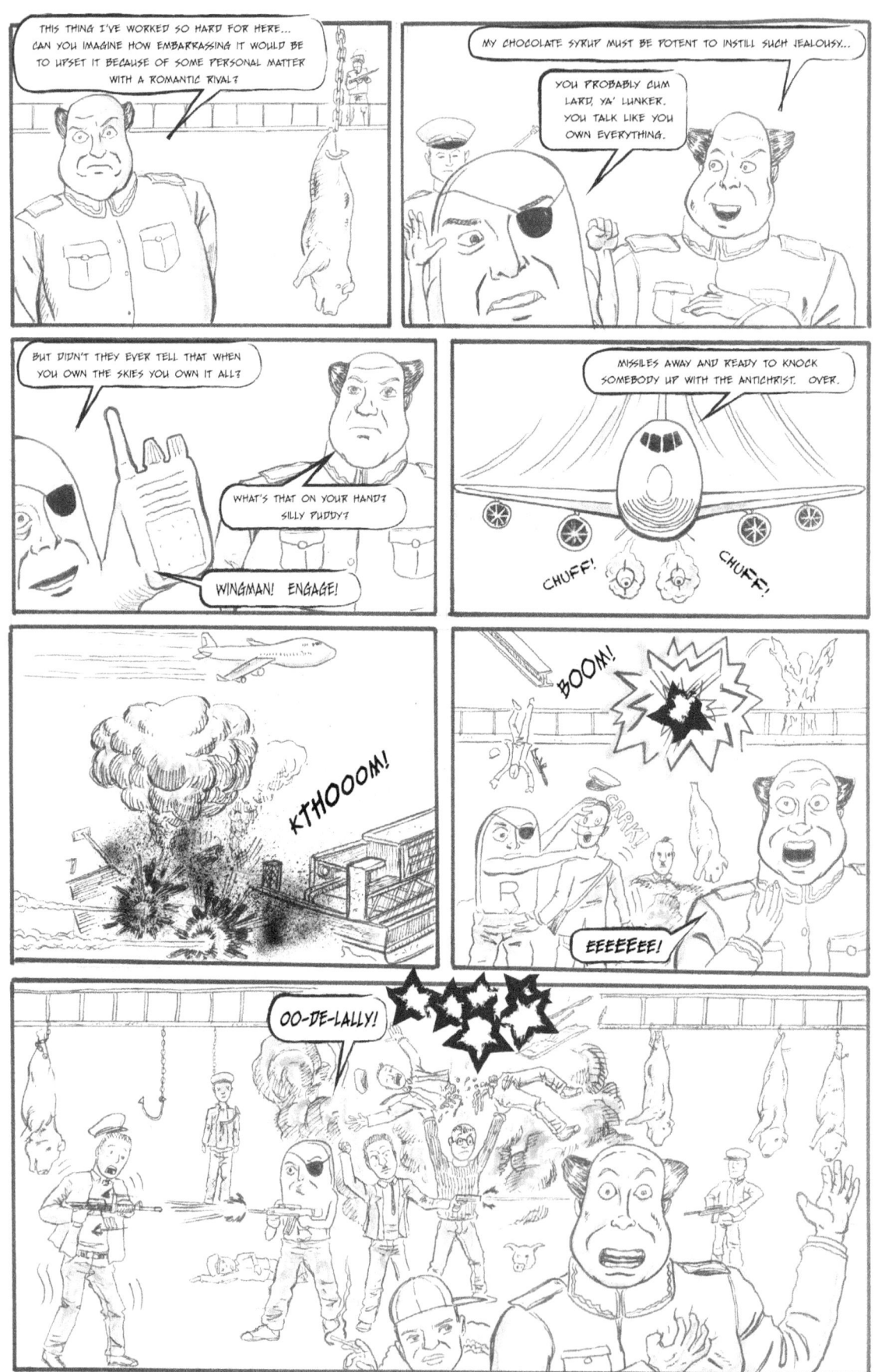

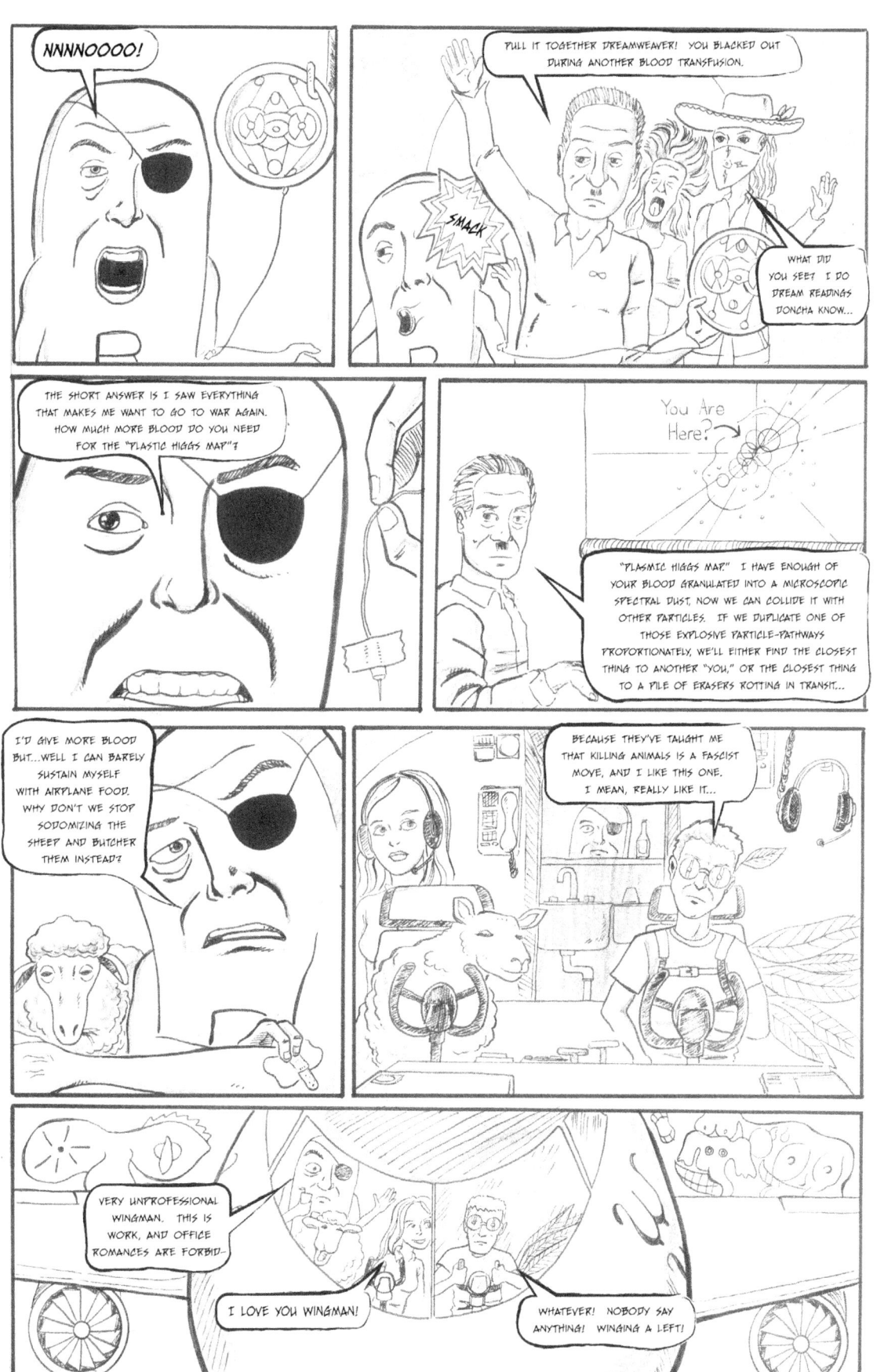

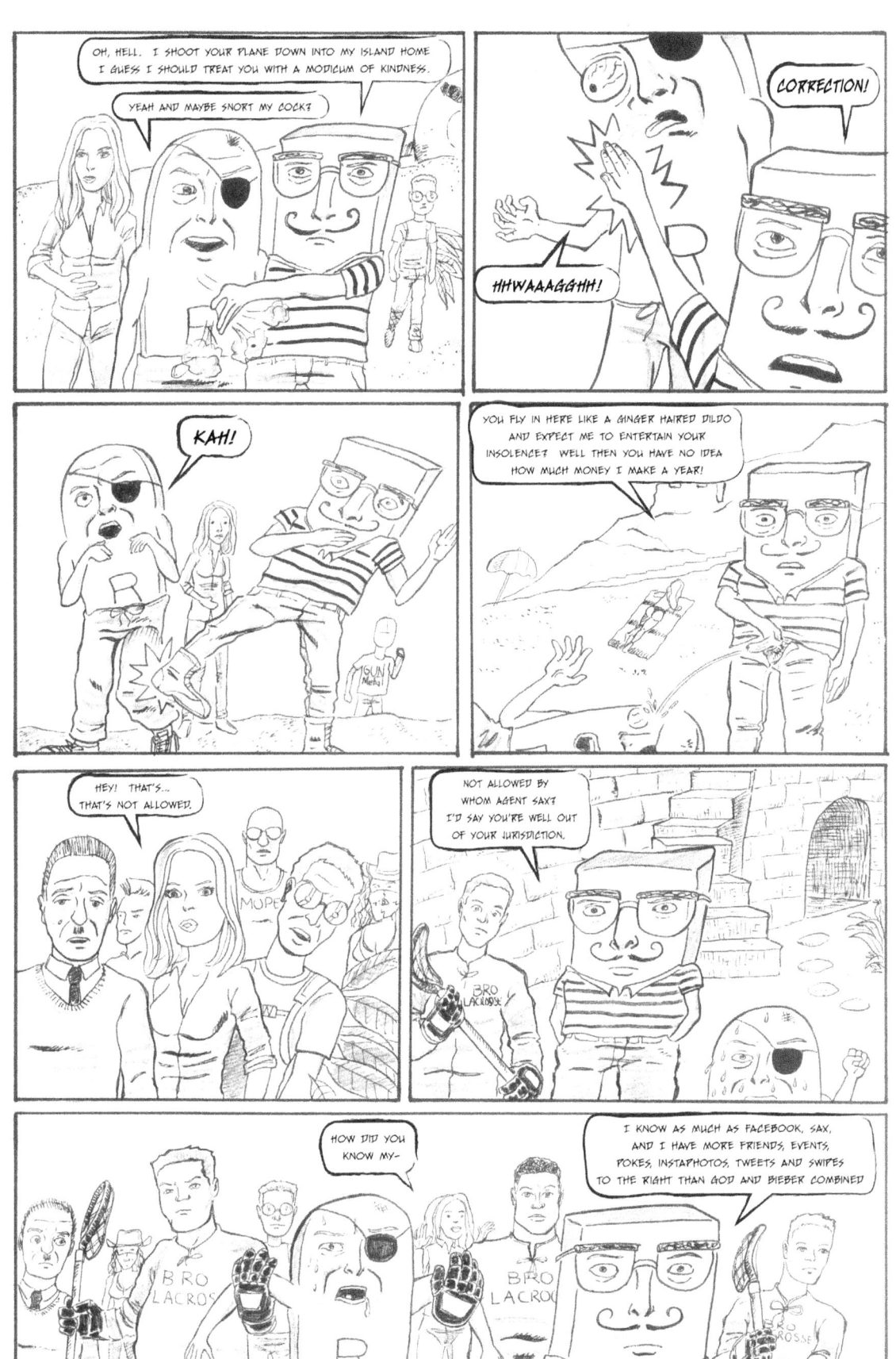

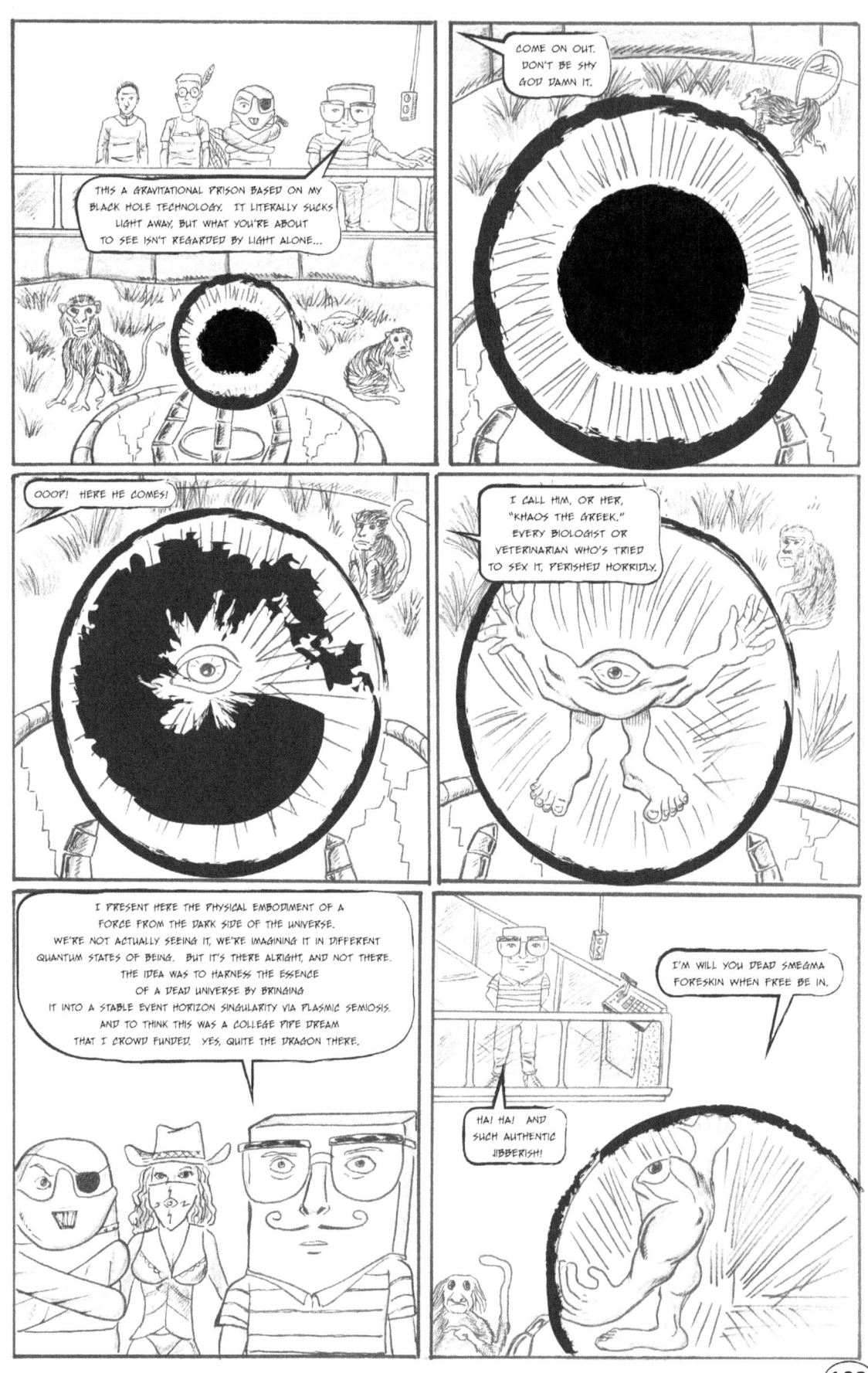

POUR YOURSELVES A GLASS OF CABERLOT AND LET'S TALK ABOUT BROADER HORIZONS.

THERE SHE IS! MY GODDESS.

PUPHHH!

OBSERVE CLARA. FOR THE FIRST TIME YOU GET TO SEE YOUR STALKER EX-BOYFRIEND AT HIS MOST EMBLEMATIC.

IS THAT- THAT MUST BE HIM. WHAT IS HE DOING HERE?

MAKING PEOPLE, ESPECIALLY HIMSELF, MISERABLE. HE STILL WANTS EVERYTHING FOR NOTHING BECAUSE HE DEEMS THE UNIVERSE TOO UNFAIR A GAME.

SO HE'S CARVED OUT AN IDENTITY THAT DOESN'T NEED TO PLAY WITH OTHERS, NO MATTER HOW INSANELY BELIGERENT IT MAY BE.

IT'S TIME HE CONSIDERED THE MERITS OF FORFEITING.

HE REMEMBERS TAKING THE SCENIC ROUTES TOWARDS THE LAND OF THE DEAD.

RECOGNIZABLE FORCES EBBING OVER THE TERRAIN LIKE A COLD FLOOD.

HIM STANDING THERE AS DARKNESS PAVES OVER WITH CONCRETE.

FORFEIT AND FORGOTTEN.

BUT FOR ANOTHER TIME. YOU WILL COME APART. AND SOMEWHERE YOU SHALL BE AGAIN.

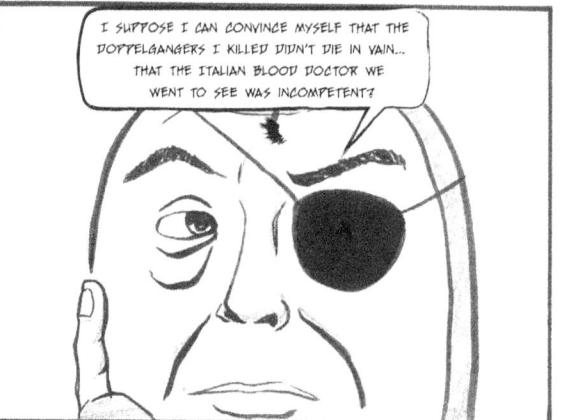

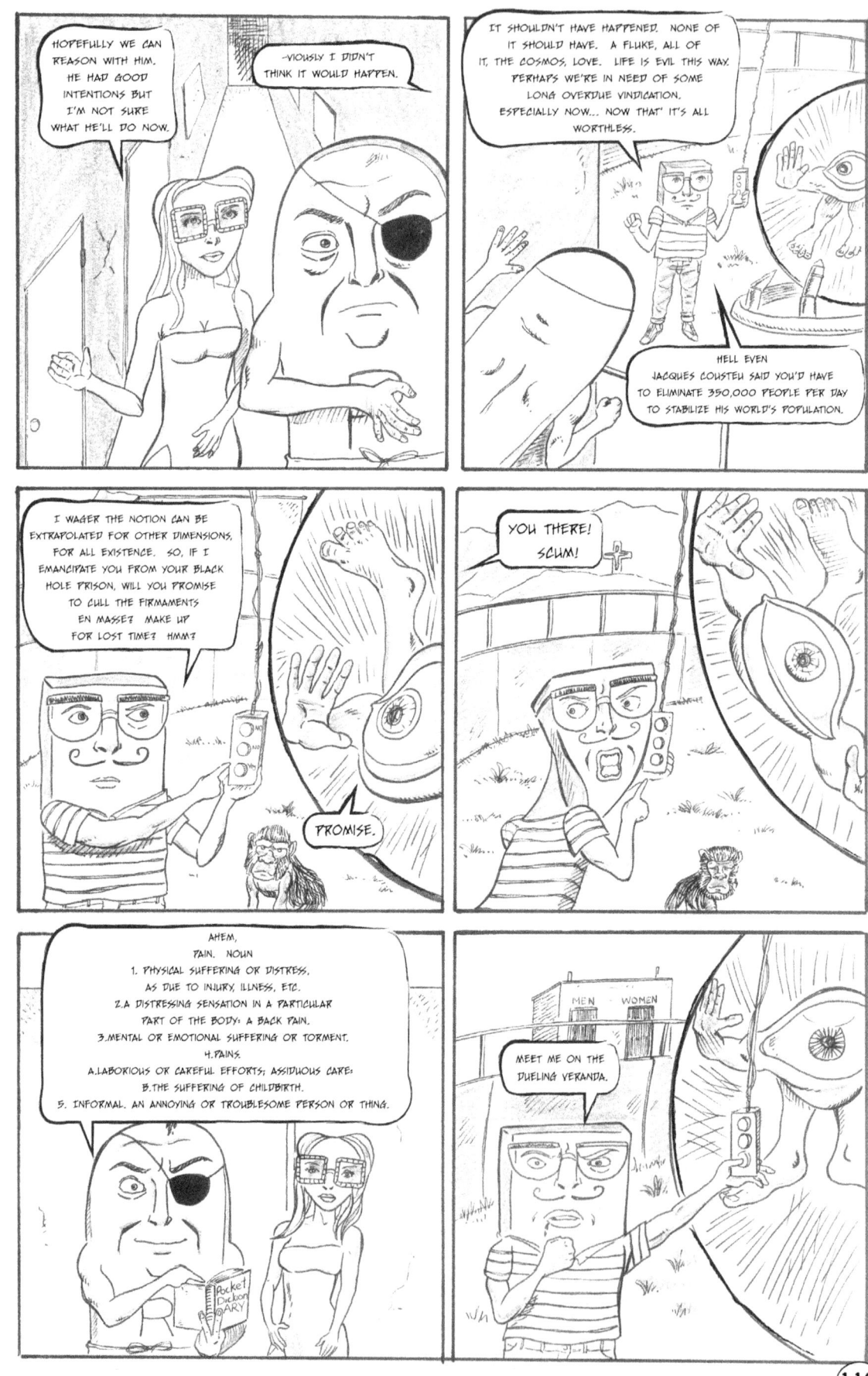

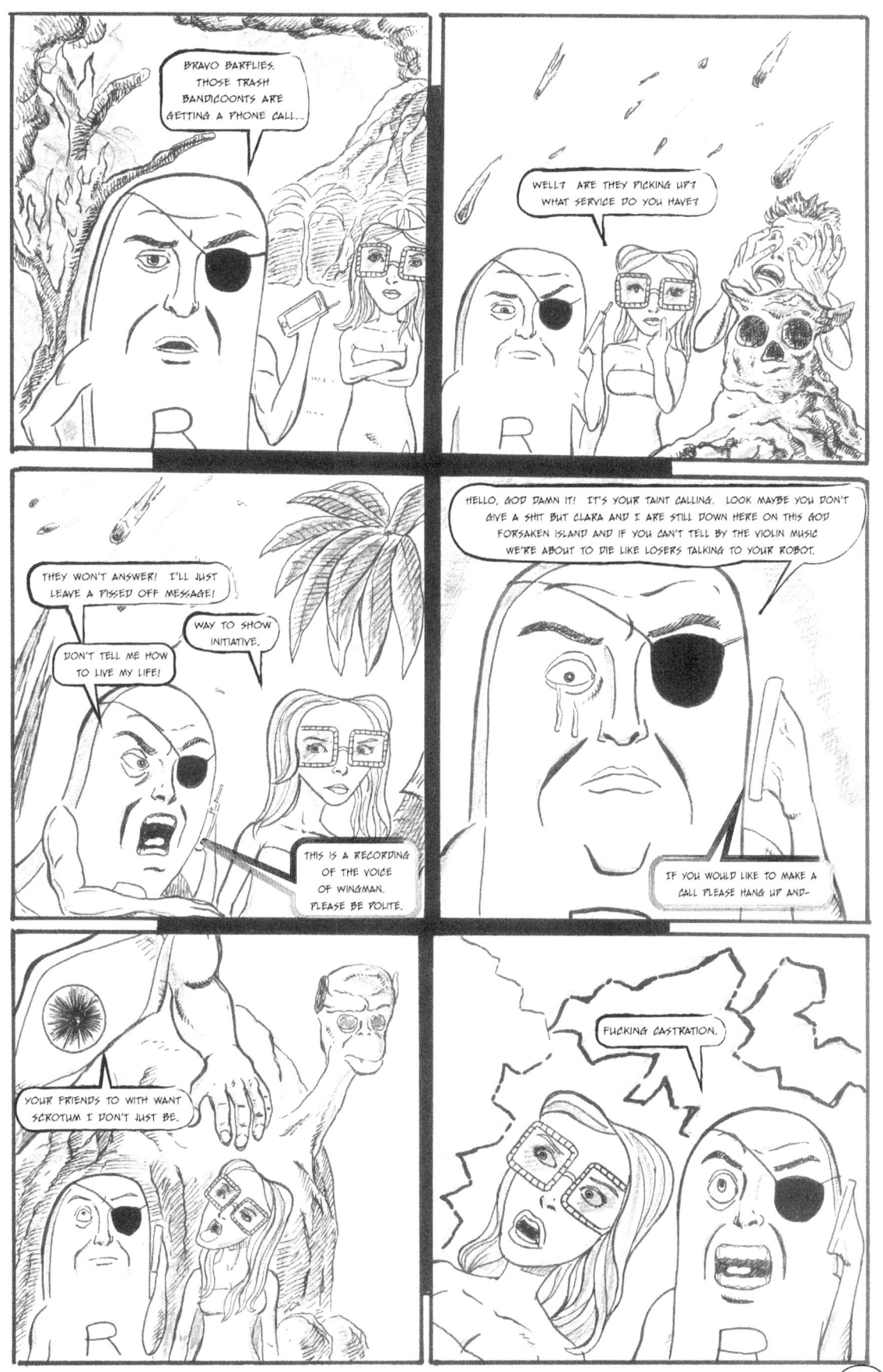

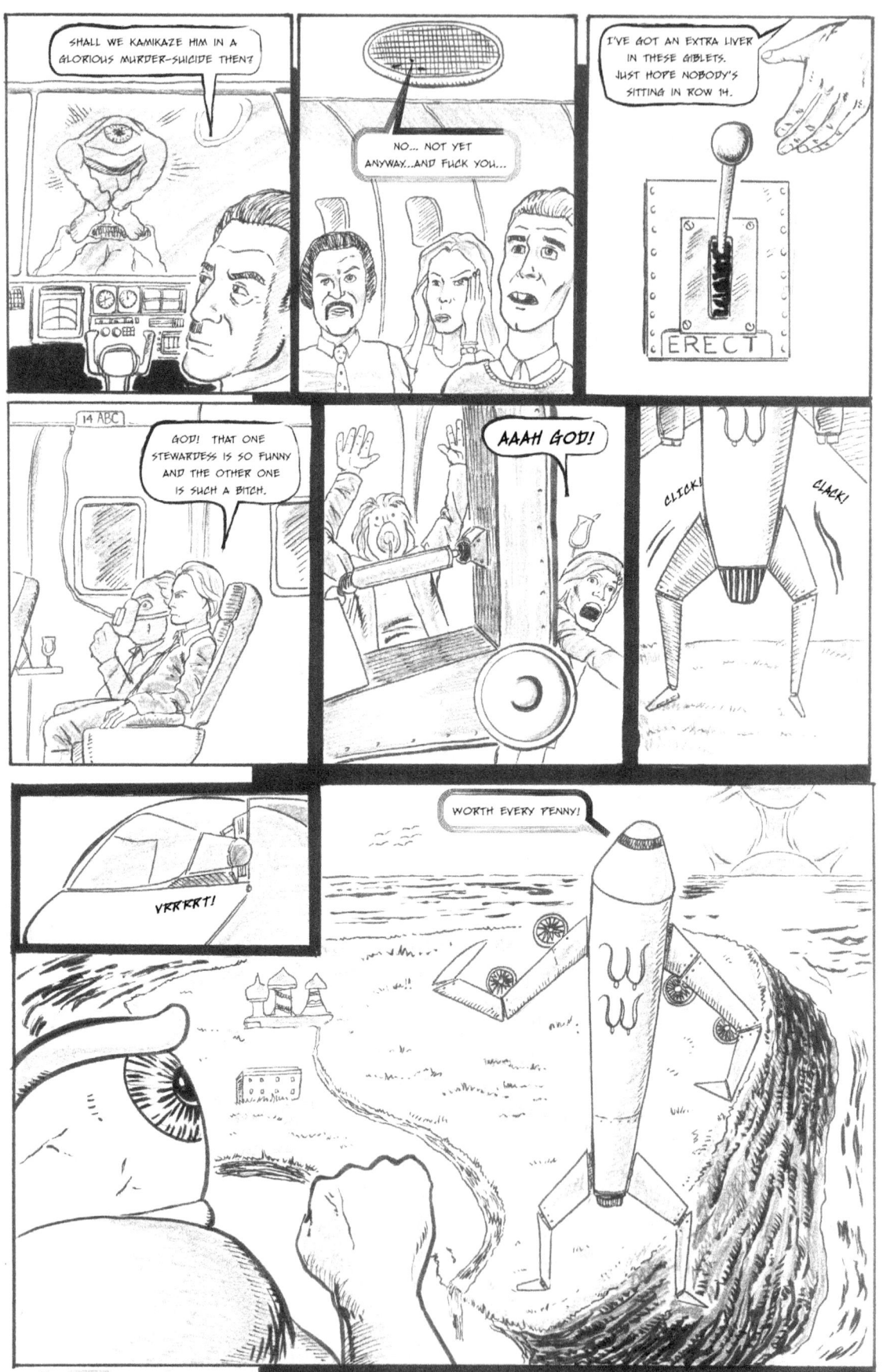

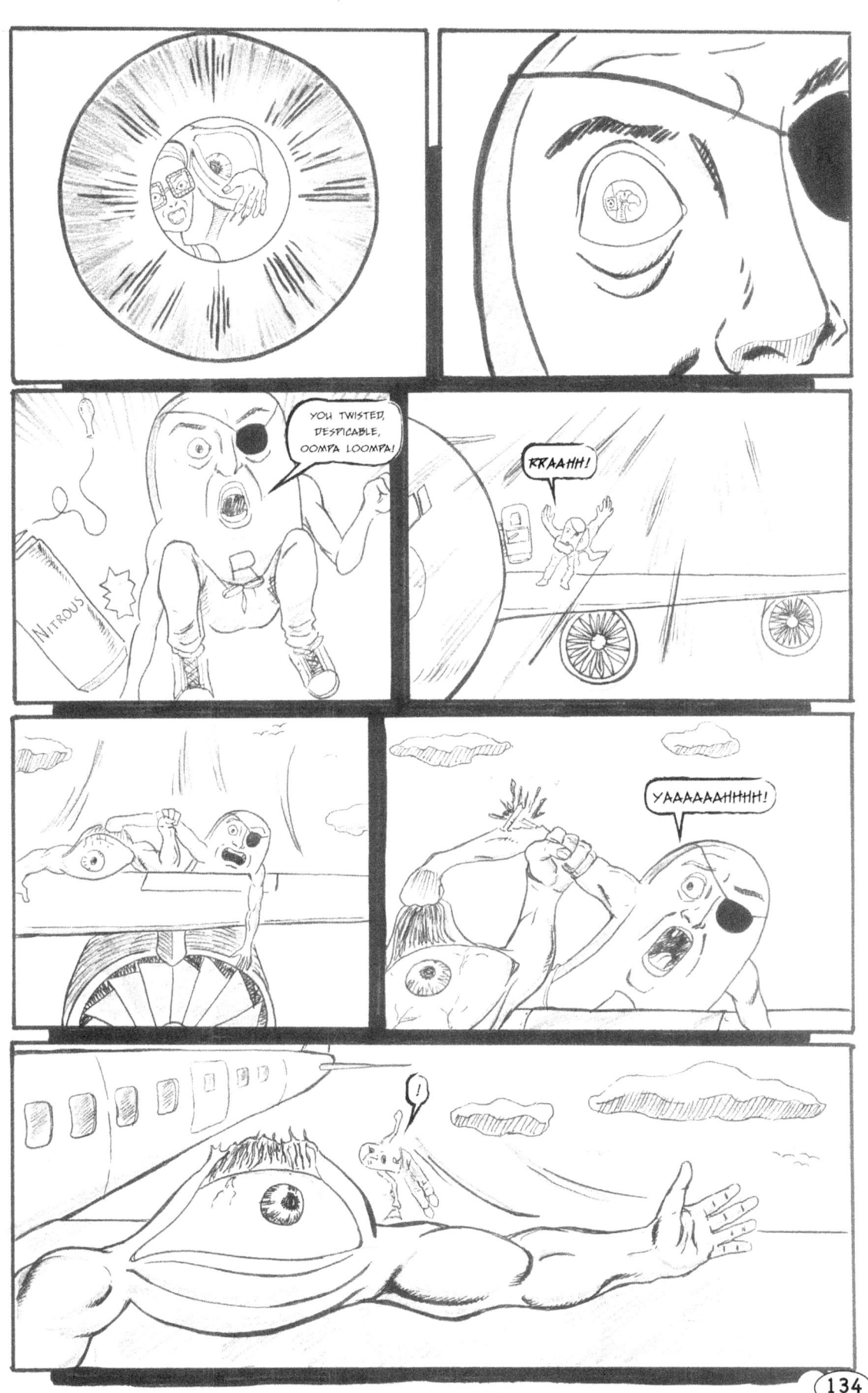

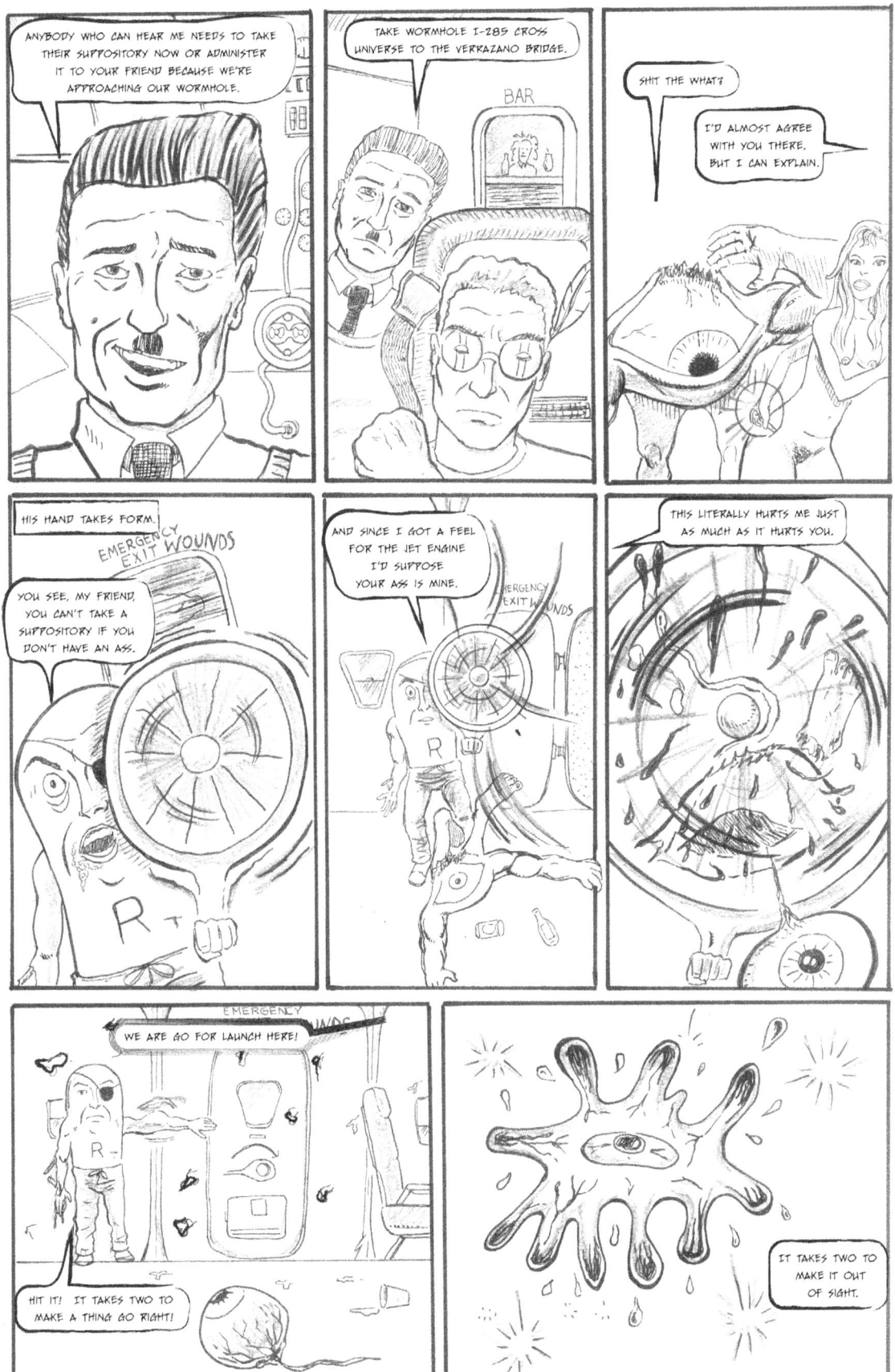

SIX MONTHS LATER...
I KNOW I WROTE YOU A LOT WHILE YOU WERE IN THE HOSPITAL AND I WAS IN PRISON BUT THIS ONE'S SPECIAL. I BURST A BLOOD VESSEL WRITING YOU THIS LETTER.
I WROTE IT AFTER ALL MY DOUBTS AND FEARS HAD ALREADY TORN US APART. FINISHED IT EVEN AFTER YOU DIDN'T WANT IT, MAYBE COULDN'T WANT IT, ANYMORE... CUZ YOU'RE DEAD.
CLARA
RUBBERMAID
??? - 2016
SOMETIMES I STILL SEE YOU IN CROWDS, PORN SITES AND OTHER STRANGE PLACES.
A WORLD OF IMAGES THAT YOU WALK IN LIKE A CLUE TO SOME DEEPER MORE SATISFYING MYSTERY IN THIS... THIS SHIT LIFE. IT'S AS THOUGH I'M ALREADY PREPARED TO SEE YOU IN DEATH!
CLARA
RUBBERMAID
??? - 2016
Whatever You Say
BOUNCES OFF OF HER
CHUFF
CLARA
RRRRRRRR
RIP
SEEING HER IN STRANGE PLACES AGAIN.
RIP
CLARA

www.ingramcontent.com/pod-product-compliance
Lightning Source LLC
Chambersburg PA
CBHW082108170626
46811CB00016B/3230

* 9 7 8 0 9 9 7 8 5 1 1 0 6 *